D1626689

Tales from
Aesop's
Fables

Tales from
Aesop's
Fables

p

This is a Parragon Book
This edition published in 2000

Parragon
Queen Street House
4 Queen Street
Bath BA1 1 HE, UK

Produced by
The Templar Company plc
Cover design by small world

ISBN 0-75254-448-9
Printed in China

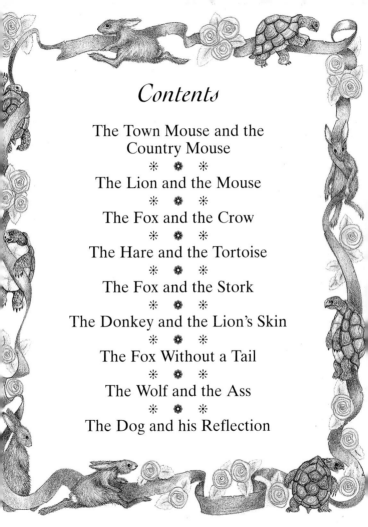

Contents

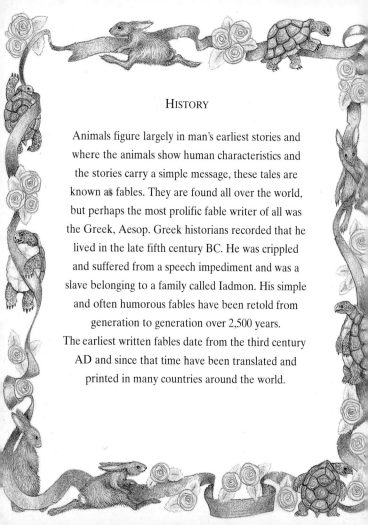

History

Animals figure largely in man's earliest stories and where the animals show human characteristics and the stories carry a simple message, these tales are known as fables. They are found all over the world, but perhaps the most prolific fable writer of all was the Greek, Aesop. Greek historians recorded that he lived in the late fifth century BC. He was crippled and suffered from a speech impediment and was a slave belonging to a family called Iadmon. His simple and often humorous fables have been retold from generation to generation over 2,500 years.

The earliest written fables date from the third century AD and since that time have been translated and printed in many countries around the world.

The Town Mouse
and the
Country Mouse

Once upon a time there were two little mice. They were cousins, but even though they came from the same family, each small mouse was very different from the other one.

One mouse lived in the town in a fine house with a butler and maids. His rooms were lined with silk and richly coloured carpets. He slept on a duck-down mattress under a velvet cover.

He wore a beautiful
embroidered waistcoat
and carried a silver-
topped cane.

Twirling his waxed moustache as he strolled along, he could never pass a mirror or shop window without first stopping to admire himself. He ate the best of foods and drank the finest wines.

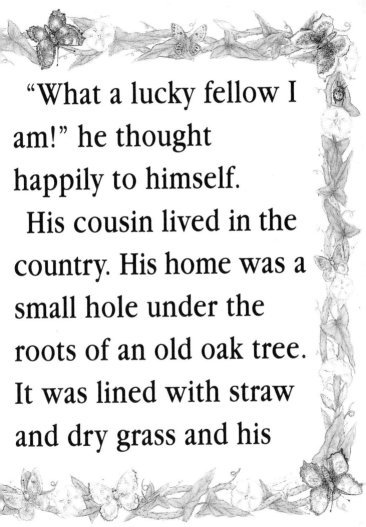

"What a lucky fellow I am!" he thought happily to himself.

His cousin lived in the country. His home was a small hole under the roots of an old oak tree. It was lined with straw and dry grass and his floor was covered with crumbling oak leaves. He slept on a scrap of dirty sheep's wool that he had found clinging to a rusty nail on the farmer's fence.

He wore a shabby old waistcoat made from an old grain sack and he carried a long crooked stick with a hooked handle which he had carved himself from the twisted twig of an old hornbeam tree.

He had never seen a mirror or a shop window in his life. He ate what food he could find in the hedgerows and used his crook to tumble blackberries from the bushes hanging overhead.

"What a lucky fellow I

am!" he thought to himself, with a smile.

One fine autumn day the Country Mouse decided he would like to share his happiness with his city cousin. He invited him to stay and busily prepared for the visit.

Soon there was a loud knock at the door.

"Welcome to my humble home," said the Country Mouse, helping his cousin off with his best silk coat. The Town Mouse looked about him with an open mouth.

"My dear chap!" he exclaimed. "How can you possibly live like this?" He pointed at the sheep's wool bed. "You can't expect me to sleep on that smelly ragbag."

"But it's warm and dry,"

replied his cousin. "What more would you want?"

The Town Mouse looked at him in astonishment but before he could speak, the Country Mouse led him to the table. There he had laid a special feast to share with his guest.

"This will cheer you up," he said encouragingly. "Look, we have a cob of corn, fresh hazelnuts, rosy red rosehips and wild blackberry juice."

The Town Mouse wrinkled his nose in disgust but politely nibbled a little at the juicy corn.

"What a terrible meal!" he thought and dabbed his whiskers with a spotted silk handkerchief.

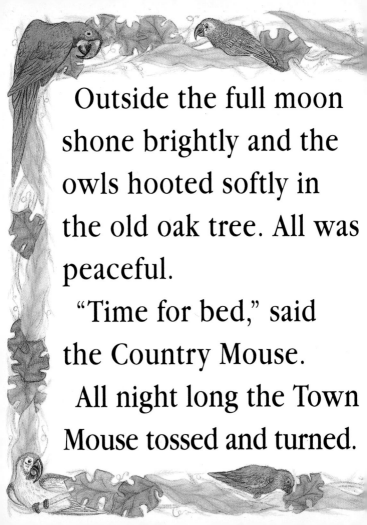

Outside the full moon shone brightly and the owls hooted softly in the old oak tree. All was peaceful.

"Time for bed," said the Country Mouse.

All night long the Town Mouse tossed and turned.

"Can you not sleep?" asked his cousin.

"It's just too QUIET!" complained the grumpy Town Mouse.

In the morning, his mind was made up.

"I am sorry, cousin," he said. "The dull country

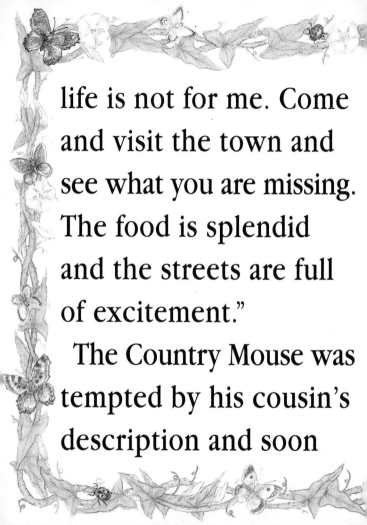

life is not for me. Come and visit the town and see what you are missing. The food is splendid and the streets are full of excitement."

The Country Mouse was tempted by his cousin's description and soon

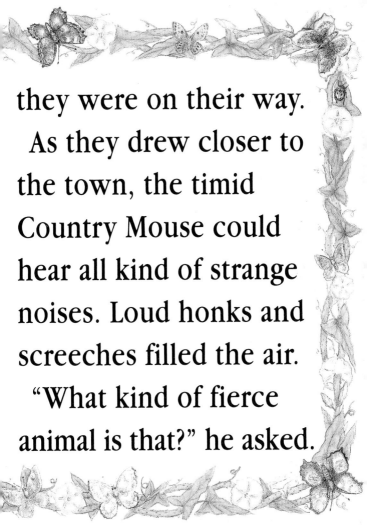

they were on their way.
As they drew closer to
the town, the timid
Country Mouse could
hear all kind of strange
noises. Loud honks and
screeches filled the air.
"What kind of fierce
animal is that?" he asked.

"That is the sound of the traffic," laughed the Town Mouse, holding his arm. "Trams and wagons, motorbikes and cars. We have them all here. You will have to keep your wits about you as we cross the road!"

In and out of the speeding wheels they dodged until at last they arrived breathless on the far pavement.

"This is terrible!" gasped the Country Mouse. "I have never been so scared in all my life!"

"You will feel safer inside," said his cousin, pulling him towards a grand house behind tall iron railings.

When they walked into the Town Mouse's home, the Country Mouse could not believe his eyes.

Never had he seen such beautiful furniture. Never had he stroked such soft silks. Never had he smelt such delicious smells!

"Come and eat," said the Town Mouse, and they scampered into the dining room. There on a long table lay a splendid banquet; whole ripe, yellow cheeses sat next to glistening mountains of brown figs.

And there was a huge
chocolate cake! The
Country Mouse darted
from dish to dish, tasting
everything at once.

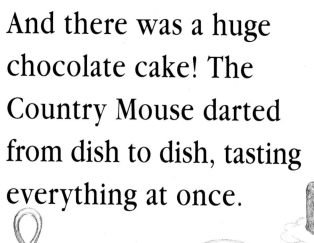

Just then the door flew open and in bounded two huge dogs. Round the table they ran, barking and growling. The two mice raced through a hole in the skirting, the dogs' long teeth snapping behind them.

Panting for breath and shaking like a leaf, the Country Mouse turned to his cousin.

"I'm going home," he squeaked. "You can enjoy the fine food and excitement of the town if you wish. But I'd

rather have my plain
and simple life in the
country and sleep safe
in my bed at night!"

MORAL:

BETTER A POOR AND SIMPLE LIFE

THAN A RICH AND WORRIED ONE.

The Lion and the Mouse

Deep in the jungle there lived a mighty Lion. He was powerful and strong with a long, golden mane and huge claws as sharp as razors.

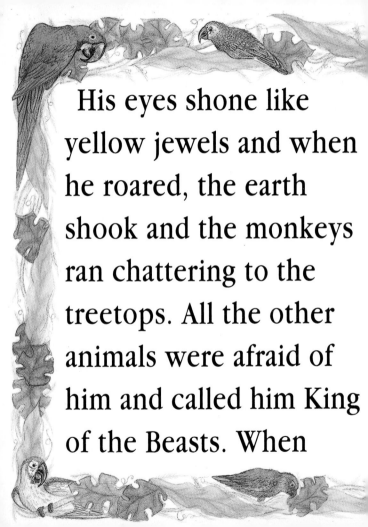

His eyes shone like yellow jewels and when he roared, the earth shook and the monkeys ran chattering to the treetops. All the other animals were afraid of him and called him King of the Beasts. When

they saw him padding
along on his enormous
paws, they quietly
slipped away and kept
safely out of sight.

The little Mouse was
especially frightened of
the Lion. She knew that
if one of his paws landed

on top of her, she would be squashed as flat as a piece of paper! When she felt the ground

tremble under his heavy tread, she would quickly scuttle to safety until he had passed by.

One day the Lion was out hunting. He chased the swift young deer, but they leapt lightly out of reach. He chased the strong young buffaloes, but they thundered away across the grassland, kicking up a great wall of dust in his face. The hyaenas laughed and cackled to see the Lion's misfortune. Slowly, he turned back and headed for the shade of an old acacia tree. There he lay down with a heavy sigh and, resting his big old head on his front paws, he slept.

The Mouse was busy about her business, searching for seeds in the grass. Under sticks and over stones she scuttled, up steep termite hills and down the other side.

Up she scurried, up,
up, up and the yellow
ground felt warm and
smooth under her
scampering paws.

Then she heard a deep
rumble and the earth
moved beneath her! Was
an earthquake on its
way? She lifted her head
and looked around. With
a shock, she realised
she had climbed onto
the Lion's back! What a

calamity! But he was
fast asleep and snoring
loudly and he didn't
seem to notice his little
visitor. Slowly the little
Mouse tiptoed down his
leg to safety. She was
near the ground when
the Lion woke up.

He could feel something tickling. In a flash, his massive paw caught the mouse in a tight grip.

"What's this?" he roared. The little Mouse could feel his hot breath on her whiskers. She nearly fainted with fright, but summoning all her courage, she squeaked loudly. The Lion looked at her in surprise.

"Oh, please have pity on me, mighty Lion," she pleaded. "Save my life and, who knows, maybe one day I will save yours."

The Lion threw back his huge head and roared with laughter.

"*You* save *my* life? A little Mouse save the King of all the Beasts? That I would certainly like to see. But you have made me laugh, little Mouse, so stop trembling and fear not, for I will not harm you."

Gently he put the little
creature down and she
scuttled for cover as soon
as her feet touched the
ground.

Now some time later,
game hunters came to
the jungle. They laid
traps for the wild animals
and all the creatures
feared them. One day,
as the great Lion prowled
along the jungle track he
heard a sudden snap and

found himself covered in something which wrapped so tightly around him that he could not move. He had been caught in a net! The more he struggled, the tighter the ropes gripped. He was trapped!

The poor Lion groaned in despair, for he knew he could not escape. Some way away, the little Mouse was busy nibbling at a tasty grass seed. She heard his cry and straightaway ran to his side.

"Once you saved my life, oh, Lion," she said, "and now I can save yours."

She sunk her sharp little teeth into the tough rope and nibbled away. Soon she had gnawed a large hole in the net and the Lion was free.

"Thank you, Mouse," he said. "Now I can see that little friends can become great friends!"

MORAL:

ONE GOOD TURN DESERVES ANOTHER.

The Fox
and the Crow

There was once a fine Fox. His pointed ears picked up the smallest sound and his sharp nose twitched at the faintest smell. All night long he prowled

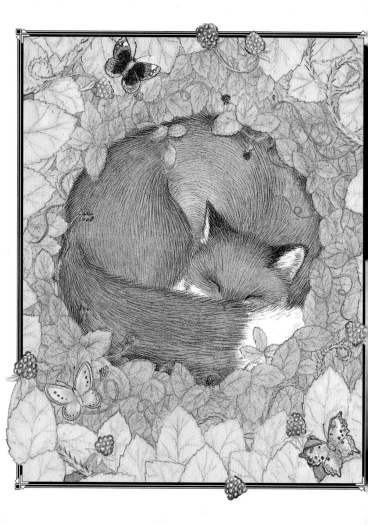

under the old oak trees, sniffing for food. As the sun came up he slunk back to his hole in a bank of brambles and, with his tail tucked over his nose, curled up and fell asleep until the day was over.

Early one evening as he crept stealthily into the wood, the Fox's sharp nose began to twitch. He could smell something interesting. Something tasty! He sniffed behind a rotten tree stump but found only a spotted

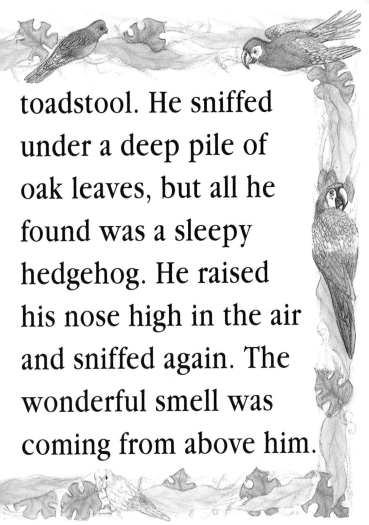

toadstool. He sniffed
under a deep pile of
oak leaves, but all he
found was a sleepy
hedgehog. He raised
his nose high in the air
and sniffed again. The
wonderful smell was
coming from above him.

He looked up and saw a Crow sitting on the branch of a large oak tree. She had a piece of cheese in her beak and it gleamed yellow in the fading light.

The Fox wanted that piece of cheese, but how was he to get it? He couldn't climb the tree. He couldn't jump high enough to reach the bird. What should he do? Then the cunning Fox had an clever idea.

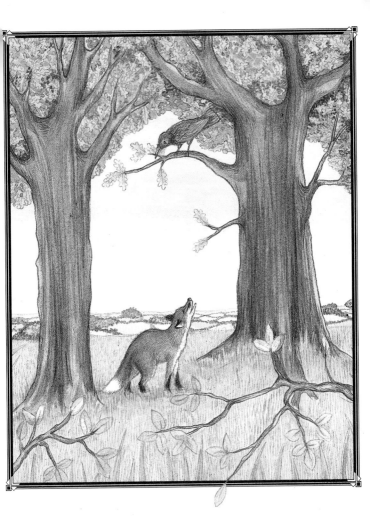

He looked up at the Crow and exclaimed, "My, what a beautiful bird! Such a golden beak!

"Such glossy black feathers! See how they shine in the evening sunlight."

The Crow was very flattered to hear all these fine compliments. No-one had ever remarked on her appearance before. She was indeed proud of her looks. She took great pains to keep her feathers trim and glossy and it was most pleasing to hear the Fox praising her beauty.

Joyfully, the crow stretched out her wings and plumped up her chest, all the while keeping a tight grip with her beak on the cheese.

"What sparkling eyes!" continued the Fox in a sugary voice. "See how they glisten like beads of jet. This is the most magnificent bird I have ever seen. I cannot believe there is a bird anywhere in the world who could match her."

The Crow fluffed up
her feathers and bobbed
up and down on the
branch, drinking in the
Fox's honeyed words.
Then the clever animal
spoke again, and his
eyes never left the large

piece of cheese.

"If only her voice was as splendid as her looks. No, it would be too much to ask. She would indeed be Queen of all the Birds if such a wondrous bird was also blessed with a glorious voice."

At this, the Crow was determined to prove herself Queen of all the Birds. She took a deep breath and gave a shrill "Caw!" The cheese tumbled from her beak and in an instant was gobbled up by the Fox.

"Well, you do have a voice, I see," smiled the Fox, licking his lips. "What a pity you don't have a brain!"

MORAL:

NEVER TRUST A FLATTERER.

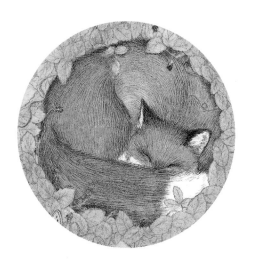

The Hare
and the
Tortoise

There once lived a bold and most bumptious Hare. He loved to strut about the warren and twirl his silken whiskers and it was evident to one and all that he obviously thought himself the finest hare in all the land. Now there was one thing that this Hare was proud of above all else. He had strong back legs and that meant that he could run faster than any other animal he had ever met.

He had the pick of the crop in the cabbage patch because he always got there before anyone else. Early in the morning, while the other sleepy Hares were still rubbing the dreams from their eyes, he would scamper up the hill to the vegetable garden, eat his fill, then scamper down again and all that could be seen of the speedy Hare was a flash of white as his fluffy cottontail bobbed by.

How he liked to race
the Rabbits and how he
loved to tease the Dogs
but no matter how hard
they tried, the Hare
beat them every time.

He was certainly a fine Hare and, with his long ears constantly twitching, he never missed a trick — or not until the day he met the Tortoise, who crawled by while the Hare was boasting to some friends.

"Ho, ho, ho!" laughed the Hare, as he caught sight of the slow-moving animal. "Come on, you old slowcoach! I hope you're in no hurry to get to where you're going. If you went any slower, you'd stop!"

The Tortoise paused and with a dignified expression, replied, "You can rush about all day long chasing your own tail if you wish, but I prefer to take my time. Why hurry?"

The Hare clicked his teeth in exasperation. "You Tortoises are all the same. Plod, plod, plod. Look at me. I run, I leap! I have places to go and people to see and I need to move fast. No time to hang about!"

The Tortoise slowly
blinked and his jaw
chewed lazily from side
to side. "I get to where

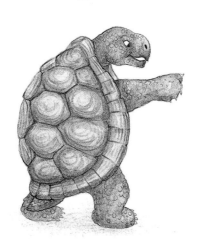

I'm going soon enough," he said. "In fact I reckon I could get there a lot faster than you."

The Hare burst into rude laughter. "Faster than me! Why, nobody runs faster than me!"

"All the same," replied the Tortoise calmly, "I challenge you to a race. Name the time and the place and I'll be there."

And so the Hare and
the Tortoise decided on
the details and the next
day everyone who was
anyone turned out to
watch the big event.

The Fox was chosen as
Umpire and he raised
his pistol high in the air.

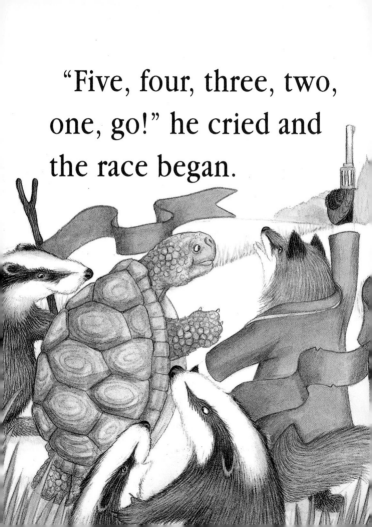

"Five, four, three, two, one, go!" he cried and the race began.

Like greased lightning
the Hare bounded away
and was soon out of
sight over the hill.

The crowd clapped and cheered. How, they asked themselves, could the poor old Tortoise hope to compete with such a natural athlete as the Hare? Why, he had hardly begun to take one step! Slowly, slowly, the cautious animal lifted first one foot and then the other and steadily made his way along the path. He looked neither to left nor right but kept his eyes on the winding road straight ahead.

On raced the Hare and the Rabbits forgot their rivalry and cheered loudly as he sped by.

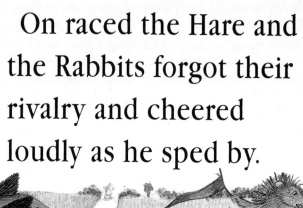

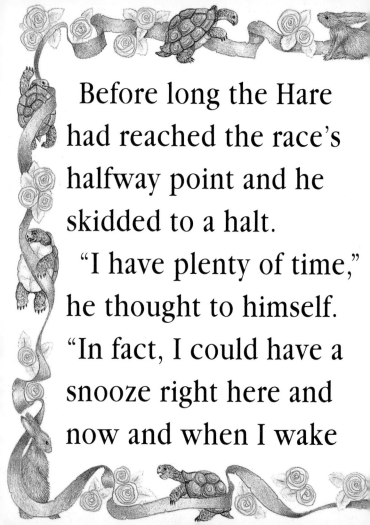

Before long the Hare had reached the race's halfway point and he skidded to a halt.

"I have plenty of time," he thought to himself. "In fact, I could have a snooze right here and now and when I wake up I would still have time to beat that Tortoise hollow!"

So saying, he sat himself down under a spreading oak tree. He leaned back and made himself comfortable and was soon fast asleep.

The hours passed and after a time over the brow of the hill could be seen the plodding Tortoise. At the same steady pace, he ambled down the hill until he reached the spot where the Hare lay fast asleep.

Silently the Tortoise observed his twitching whiskers and without breaking his step carried on down the dusty road.

The sun moved across the sky and still the Hare slept. Every now and then a paw trembled as he chased butterflies in his dreams.

On plodded the steady Tortoise, looking neither to left nor right, but just straight ahead with one goal in mind as the sun began to sink in the sky.

The air grew cooler and the Hare suddenly awoke with a shiver. He looked back down the road. No Tortoise in sight. Well, no surprise there, thought the Hare and with a satisfied grunt, the speedy animal was once again on his way. Up hill and down dale he raced and soon the finish line was in sight. But why was everyone cheering? They could at least wait for him to cross the tape! Then he saw the Tortoise.

He was only inches from the ribbon and, as the Hare raced after him, his shiny shell snapped it in two.

As the Hare panted for breath at the end of the race, the Tortoise smiled placidly.

"Slow I may be but I keep my eye on the goal and I don't let anything distract me!"

MORAL: SLOW AND STEADY WINS THE RACE

The Fox
and the Stork

One day a Fox decided to invite a Stork to tea. He dressed in his best suit and set the table nicely.

Soon there was a tap, tap, tap upon the door.

It was the Stork's beak gently knocking and with a great flourish, the Fox threw the door wide, bowed low and invited her to step inside.

"Welcome to my very humble abode," he cried. "Let us eat!"

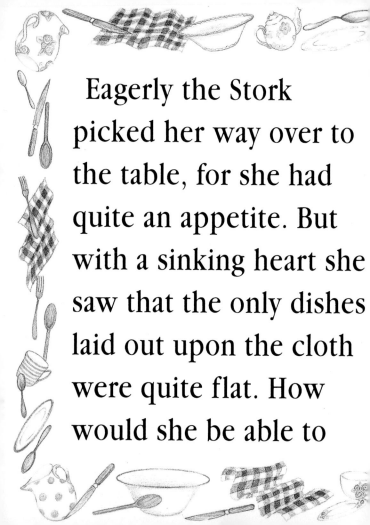

Eagerly the Stork picked her way over to the table, for she had quite an appetite. But with a sinking heart she saw that the only dishes laid out upon the cloth were quite flat. How would she be able to eat off such a plate?

In bustled the Fox from the kitchen with a steaming pan of soup and with much smacking of lips and a great many appreciative sniffs, he ladled out a good portion into each plate.

"Bon appetit!" the Fox exclaimed, smiling broadly at the Stork. Dismayed, she looked down at her plate.

It did smell good, but with her long beak she was scarcely able to drink a drop.

Greedily, the Fox lapped up his plateful and then looked over at the Stork's dish which was hardly touched.

"Did you not enjoy the soup? Did I add too much salt and pepper for your liking?" he asked, wrinkling his brow as if greatly concerned. But the poor Stork was too polite to comment.

Then the Fox ate her portion as well.

That night the hungry Stork lay awake for a long time listening to the rumblings of her empty stomach, but the cunning Fox slept like a baby and dreamt of great lakes full of tasty soup. The next day when the Stork awoke she was still hungry. She decided to repay the Fox's hospitality and invite him to dinner. He was delighted and accepted eagerly.

With a loud rat-a-tat-tat
the Fox rapped upon
her door with his silver-
topped cane.

Bowing her head gracefully, she welcomed him inside. Soon they were both sitting down to eat but the Fox could scarcely believe his eyes when he saw that the only pots upon the table were two tall jugs.

"I do hope you enjoy your soup," smiled the Stork. "Bon appetit!"

Then she dipped her slender beak into the neck of the jug and drank away until not a drop was left. But the Fox sat dumbstruck.

He could only lick his lips hungrily and watch while she happily finished her meal.

He returned home a sadder and wiser fox with nobody to blame but himself for, as he plainly realised, he had only been paid back for his own uncaring behaviour.

MORAL: DO AS YOU WOULD BE DONE BY

The Donkey in the Lion's Skin

There was once an unhappy Donkey. He lived in a jungle with a Lion, a Tiger, a Fox, a Wolf, a Monkey and a Bear — but they were all quite unfriendly.

The cruel creatures often made fun of him. "Big ears!" they would call from the tangled thorn thickets.

"Clodhopper! Call that a tail?" shrieked the Monkey. "I've seen better Rat's tails!"

The poor Donkey just hung his head in shame. How he longed to show them that he, too, could be brave and strong. But whenever he tried to join in their games he was turned away and no matter how hard he tried to be friendly, the other animals would only laugh at him and call him names.

And so he kept himself to himself and the jungle animals left him alone and nobody paid him any attention at all.

One day a hunter came to the jungle. Before he had taken one step under the great canopy, the animals could sense he was there.

All twittering and chattering ceased and a heavy silence fell on the trees. Warily the hunter looked to right and left, then shouldering his gun, he prowled under the branches and through the twisted creepers that hung down in his path.

Slowly the Monkeys began to chatter with fear and before long the whole forest was loudly shrieking its alarm. With pattering feet, the timid animals ran and hid.

But one great beast refused to move. He yawned, scratched and went back to sleep. This was the great Lion, King of the Jungle. *He* was not going to be scared off like some nervous little Mouse.

The Monkey ran shrieking to the very top of a tall tree. The Wolf slunk beneath a bush in the dappled shade. The Tiger lay flat along a wide branch and the Bear lumbered back to his lair.

But the Lion yawned, and yawned again and, laying his great shaggy head on his front paws, he slept on. The other animals were afraid of the Lion and so they left him alone to fend for himself.

So it was that the Hunter found him, as he crept silently through the heart of the jungle. Slowly he raised his gun and aimed at the sleeping Lion. Bang! went the shot and the Monkeys screamed in the tree tops.

The Lion lay dead and in a trice the Hunter had skinned him and set off for home with the meat upon his back. The Lion's tawny skin lay on the jungle floor for many weeks and not a creature went near.

But one day along came the Donkey and what a fright he got when he first saw the skin for he thought it was the Lion, still fast asleep! "This would make a fine costume for me to wear!" he said.

Carefully he slipped the skin over his back. There was a lake nearby and as he bent over to admire his reflection in the water he jumped back in surprise for he looked exactly like a real Lion!

"Now I can teach those animals a lesson," he said to himself and he hid in a thicket and waited for someone to pass by. Soon the noisy Monkeys came swinging along, clinging to the vines with their tails.

Out from the thicket jumped the Donkey, shaking his Lion's head from side to side. The Monkeys screeched with fear and scrambled up the tree trunks to safety. The Donkey stamped his hooves with glee!

Soon the Bear came ambling along the path, following the buzzing honeybees to their hive. Out leapt the Donkey and the terrified Bear turned heel and ran off into the bushes with a frightened whimper.

After a while the fierce Tiger came prowling by but as soon as he saw the Donkey in the Lion's skin, he ran off as fast as he could. The happy Donkey had never had so much fun in all his life!

So he spent many happy hours playing tricks on all the animals who had caused him so much unhappiness and not one of them ever guessed that under the fierce Lion skin was the humble Donkey.

The sun was slowly sinking in the west as the crafty Fox slunk into view, sniffing and snouting for food. Out rushed the Donkey and to his great delight the terrified Fox yelped and ran for cover.

But this time the silly Donkey could not help himself and he laughed out loud. His loud bray echoed through the jungle and the wily Fox stood still.

Slowly the Fox walked back to the fierce Lion skin and looked under the great head. There he came face to face with the embarrassed Donkey who hung his head low and blushed. The Fox laughed aloud.

"You foolish Donkey! If only you had kept your mouth shut, your trick might well have succeeded but you had to give yourself away with your loud bray!"

MORAL: A FOOL MAY DECEIVE OTHERS WITH HIS APPEARANCE BUT HIS WORDS WILL SOON REVEAL HIM.

The Fox
Without a Tail

There was once a fine Fox, a most handsome fellow with a shiny red coat, beady black eyes and a long bushy tail. Indeed, he was a rather vain creature and his house was full of mirrors.

Every morning he would gaze at his reflection and admire his good looks and every night he would take out his bristle brush and stroke his long tail from top to tip until it shone like copper.

He spent his evenings
prowling through
thickets and hunting
along the hedgerows.

All the small animals were quick to get out of the way of his sharp snuffling nose and his strong white teeth. Under the oak trees he slunk like a shadow and the leaves shivered as he passed by.

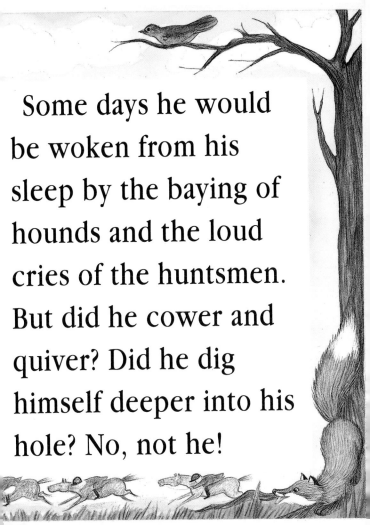

Some days he would be woken from his sleep by the baying of hounds and the loud cries of the huntsmen. But did he cower and quiver? Did he dig himself deeper into his hole? No, not he!

This bold fox would
snap at their noses until
the poor dogs tucked
their tails between their
legs and fled.

One cool evening, as the silver moon hung low above the horizon, the hungry Fox was out hunting for rabbits and any other tasty morsels that might be unlucky enough to come his way.

Around the warren he crept on silent paws and deep in their holes the frightened creatures shook with fear.

But the Fox was so busy concentrating on on being the hunter, that he forgot one thing.

He, too, could be hunted! Suddenly a loud *snap*! broke the silence and the Fox felt a terrible pain.

Twisting round he saw
that his fine full tail had
been caught in an iron
trap! The sharp teeth
squeezed tightly on the
thick red fur and the
poor Fox howled in
agony. This way and
that he twisted in a

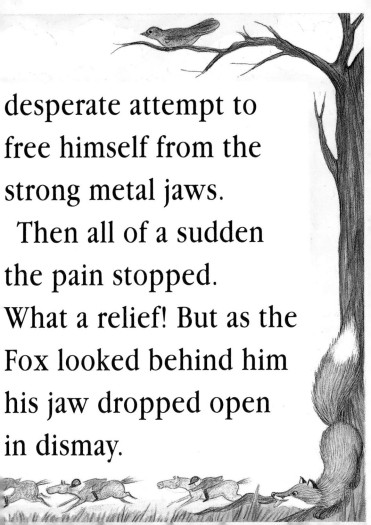

desperate attempt to
free himself from the
strong metal jaws.
   Then all of a sudden
the pain stopped.
What a relief! But as the
Fox looked behind him
his jaw dropped open
in dismay.

The trap had pulled his
tail clean off and there
it lay in all its glory
upon the ground.

The Fox's relief was quickly replaced with anger and deep shame. How could he possibly face all the other animals without a tail? Why, he was a Fox! The best and finest Fox that ever was!

And what was a Fox without his tail? He would never be able to hold his head high again. He could almost hear the other animals' cruel laughter as they watched him creeping by without his beautifu

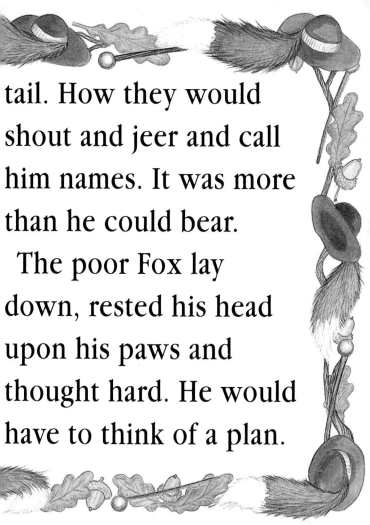

tail. How they would shout and jeer and call him names. It was more than he could bear.

The poor Fox lay down, rested his head upon his paws and thought hard. He would have to think of a plan.

He thought and thought and by the time the moon was high in the sky he had decided what he should do.

Every night at midnight the Foxes would meet in the forest dell to discuss any grievances or complaints they might have. There they all sat in a circle as the moon shadows spread over the ground.

With his head held high, the Fox slowly walked into the centre of the circle as a hushed silence fell all around.

He was wearing his best hat and tucked inside the hatband was his own fine red tail! Proudly he strutted before them and at last sat down on a bare rock. Very quietly a young Fox began to

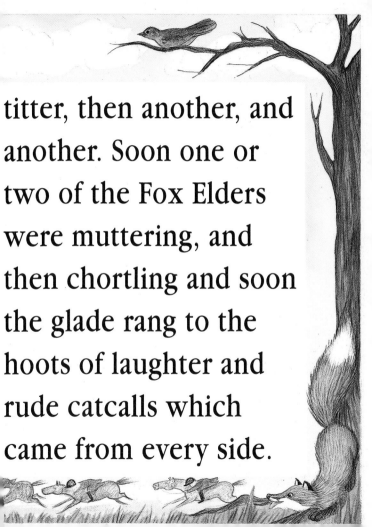

titter, then another, and another. Soon one or two of the Fox Elders were muttering, and then chortling and soon the glade rang to the hoots of laughter and rude catcalls which came from every side.

But the Fox simply
lifted his nose even
higher in the air and
waited for the noise
to die down.

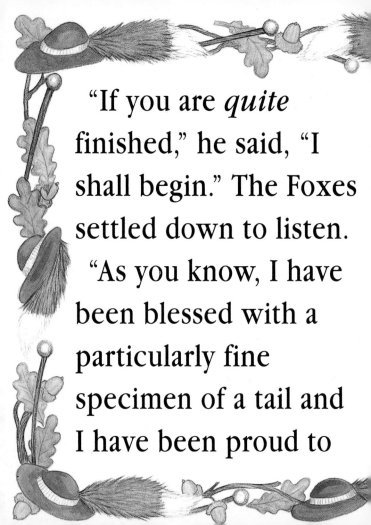

"If you are *quite* finished," he said, "I shall begin." The Foxes settled down to listen.

"As you know, I have been blessed with a particularly fine specimen of a tail and I have been proud to

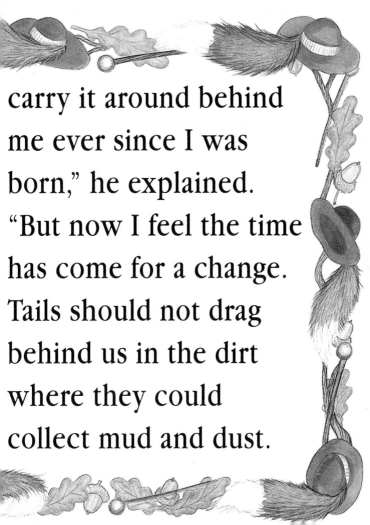

carry it around behind
me ever since I was
born," he explained.
"But now I feel the time
has come for a change.
Tails should not drag
behind us in the dirt
where they could
collect mud and dust.

"Tails should be worn in the hat, like so," and he gracefully inclined his head the better to show off his fine plumage. There was a shocked silence in the glade. "From now on I propose that all us

Foxes should remove our tails from our rear ends and wear them in our hats," he continued. The Foxes looked at one another in complete amazement. The Fox stood up and cleared his throat.

"I am renowned throughout the land as a leader of fashion and you would all be well-advised to follow my trend unless you wish to appear hopelessly out of date."

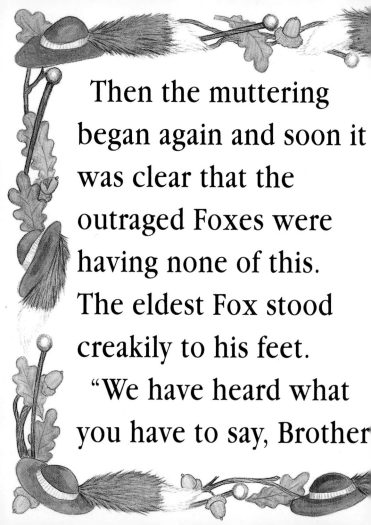

Then the muttering began again and soon it was clear that the outraged Foxes were having none of this. The eldest Fox stood creakily to his feet.

"We have heard what you have to say, Brother

Fox," he said politely, "and it seems quite clear to me what has happened, but could you be so kind as to answer me this?" The other Foxes nudged one another in eager anticipation.

"Would you be so very keen to change the fashion and have us all wear our tails upon our heads if you had not lost your own tail in a *trap*?"

Then the poor Fox
realised that everyone
had seen through his
clever plan and they
were not to be
persuaded. He hung
his head in shame and
slunk away into the
deepest depths of the

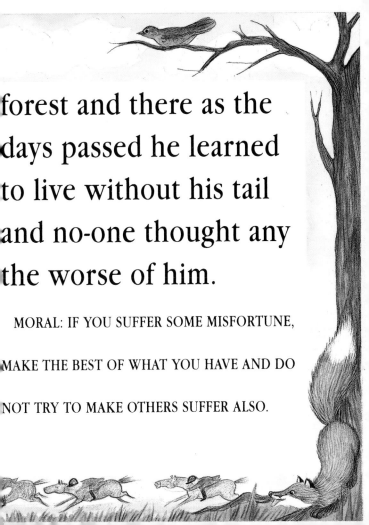

forest and there as the days passed he learned to live without his tail and no-one thought any the worse of him.

MORAL: IF YOU SUFFER SOME MISFORTUNE, MAKE THE BEST OF WHAT YOU HAVE AND DO NOT TRY TO MAKE OTHERS SUFFER ALSO.

The Wolf and the Ass

The Ass was cross. The other animals had been teasing the Donkey, and because the Ass was the Donkey's cousin, they had been making fun of him, too.

Now it has to be said that the Donkey was not the cleverest of animals. He would happily spend hours passing the time of day with his reflection in the pond and he had long conversations with his shadow, who trotted along companionably at his side.

But the Ass was quite a different matter. He was crafty and cunning and considered himself a far superior animal to his lowly cousin.

He was greatly offended that the other animals should treat him so badly. "One day they will discover that I am nobody's fool," he promised himself.

Some weeks later the Ass was busy nibbling at the tender thistles that grew down by the riverbank. The sun shone from a cloudless sky and the only sounds to be heard were the steady chomping of his

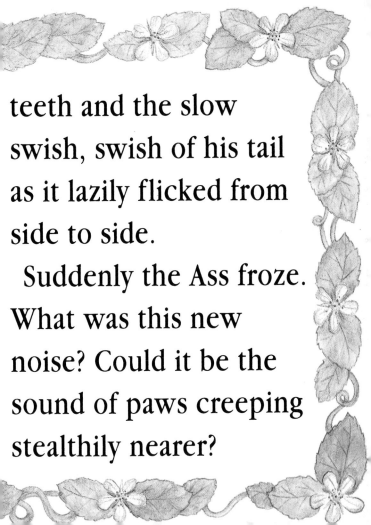

teeth and the slow
swish, swish of his tail
as it lazily flicked from
side to side.

Suddenly the Ass froze.
What was this new
noise? Could it be the
sound of paws creeping
stealthily nearer?

The Ass listened
intently but all was
silent and still. Slowly
he lowered his head
and continued to graze.

But just a few seconds later the Ass froze again. This time there was no mistake and the hair on his back prickled all the way from his long ears right down to his tail. Nervously he looked over his shoulder.

There in the bushes he saw the unmistakeable gleam of the big grey Wolf's shining eyes.

"That Wolf plans to make me his supper," thought the Ass. "I must

do something." Soon he had thought of a clever plan to save himself.

The Ass moved off in search of more thistles but now he limped as he went along. He hobbled slowly as the Wolf crept like a shadow behind him.

The Ass began to chew a fresh clump of thistles.

all the time watching the Wolf from the corner of his eye. The Wolf prowled nearer and nearer and his tongue hung so low he almost tripped over it. Soon he was close enough to pounce.

"I shouldn't do that if I was you," called out the Ass quite calmly. The Wolf started, quite astonished to find the Ass so unafraid.

"I have trodden on a sharp thorn," explained the Ass, "and if you eat me, it will be sure to stick in your throat."

The Wolf sat down and thought about this unexpected problem. He was very hungry but he certainly didn't want to run the risk of choking on a thorn. Then the Ass spoke again. "I will lift up my hoof," he said helpfully, "and then you can pull out the thorn. I would hate it to hurt you."

"This Ass really *is* foolish," thought the Wolf with a sly grin.

The Ass lifted his leg and the Wolf examined the hoof carefully, but there was no thorn to be found! Then the Ass summoned up all his strength and gave a mighty kick. With a howl of pain, the Wolf flew head over heels high into the air and landed with a thump in a bush of prickly thistles!

He stumbled painfully to his feet as the Ass galloped away with a loud whinny of triumph.

The Wolf shook his head ruefully. That Ass was certainly not as silly as he looked!

MORAL: BEWARE OF UNEXPECTED FAVOURS

The Dog and his Reflection

There was once a naughty Dog. He was always hungry and no matter how large a meal he ate, he always had room for one or two bites more.

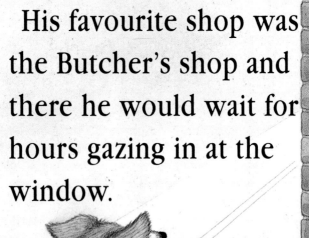

His favourite shop was
the Butcher's shop and
there he would wait for
hours gazing in at the
window.

He admired the long strings of glistening pink sausages. He praised the plump pork chops. He bowed down before the brisket of beef. Come rain or shine, the Dog would sit happily all day long

watching the Butcher
at his work. But the
Butcher did not like to
see the Dog.

"Be off!" he would cry.
"I have no meat for you!"
Then the Dog would
slink away with his tail
between his legs.

One day the Dog woke up and looked at his empty larder in dismay. "Time to find some food," he said. Soon he was at the Butcher's shop and there in the window was the most wonderful ham bone!

The Dog sniffed longingly. He wanted that bone! As soon as the Butcher's back was turned, the Dog saw his chance. In a flash he put his paws upon the counter and seized the bone in his mouth.

Then he was away
down the street leaving
the Butcher far behind
him, shouting angrily
and waving his sharpest
knife!

The Dog trotted along well pleased with himself. Nobody had a bone as big and as tasty as his! But as he crossed the bridge over the stream something caught his eye. There below him was another

Dog and to his dismay, this other Dog was also carrying a bone. And this bone was just as big and just as tasty as his own! Angrily the Dog snarled over the bridge. The other Dog snarled back.

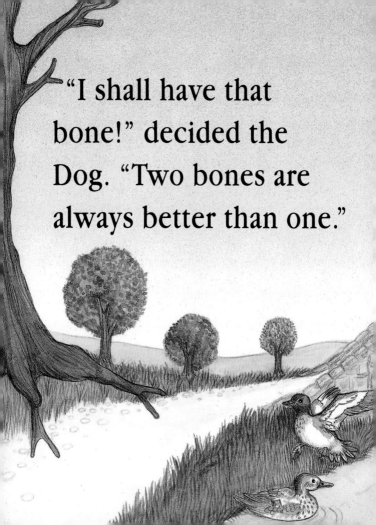

"I shall have that bone!" decided the Dog. "Two bones are always better than one."

With that, the silly dog opened his mouth and snapped greedily. But what a shock he had when his own bone tumbled from his mouth and landed with a loud splash in the water.

Quickly it sank out of sight and the Dog whimpered sadly. "I was wrong," he sighed. "One bone is better than none."

MORAL: BE GRATEFUL FOR WHAT YOU HAVE